Digger Pig
and the
Turnip

Digger Pig
and the
Turnip

Caron Lee Cohen
Illustrated by Christopher Denise

Green Light Readers
Harcourt, Inc.
San Diego   New York   London

First Green Light Readers edition 2000
Green Light Readers is a registered trademark of Harcourt, Inc.

Library of Congress Cataloging-in-Publication Data
Cohen, Caron Lee.
Digger Pig and the turnip/Caron Lee Cohen; illustrated by Christopher Denise.
—1st Green Light Readers ed.
p. cm.
"Green Light Readers."
Summary: In this adaptation of a traditional folktale, a dog, duck, and chick refuse
to help a pig prepare a turnip pie but nevertheless expect to eat it when it's ready.
[1. Folklore.] I. Denise, Christopher, ill. II. Title.
PZ8.1.C66455Di 2000
398.24'52—dc21   99-6802
ISBN 0-15-202524-3
ISBN 0-15-202530-8 (pb)

C E G H F D B

C E G H F D B (pb)

One day Digger Pig dug up a big turnip.
"I can use this to make a good turnip pie,"
she said.

Chirper Chick, Quacker Duck, and Bow-Wow Dog sat around in their corner of the barn.

"Let's make a turnip pie," said Digger Pig. "Who will help me cut the turnip?"

"Not I," said Chirper Chick.
"Not I," said Quacker Duck.
"Not I," said Bow-Wow Dog.

"All right then. I will cut the turnip myself," said Digger Pig.

And she did.

Then Digger Pig asked, "Who will help me mash the turnip?"

"Not I," said Chirper Chick.
"Not I," said Quacker Duck.
"Not I," said Bow-Wow Dog.

"All right then. I will mash the turnip myself," said Digger Pig.

And she did.

Next, Digger Pig asked, "Who
will help me make the pie?"

"Not I," said Chirper Chick.
"Not I," said Quacker Duck.
"Not I," said Bow-Wow Dog.

"All right then. I will make the pie myself!" said Digger Pig.

And she did.
She called her piglets to supper.

"Can we have some pie?" the others asked. "No!" grunted Digger Pig. "You didn't help. My piglets and I will eat it all."

And they did!

Meet the Illustrator

Christopher Denise likes drawing animals. Before he starts to draw, he looks at pictures of real animals to get ideas. He says, "I know children will like a story even more if the animals are really special."